W9-ALV-553

DISCARD

JUST GOING TO THE DENTIST

BY
MERCER MAYER

For Len, Jessie,
Arden & Benjamin
My Wonderful Children
who have and will make
our dentist rich.

A GOLDEN BOOK · NEW YORK

Just Going to the Dentist book, characters, text, and images © 1990 Mercer Mayer. LITTLE CRITTER, MERCER MAYER'S LITTLE CRITTER, and MERCER MAYER'S LITTLE CRITTER and Logo are registered trademarks of Orchard House Licensing Company. All rights reserved under International and Pan-American Copyright Conventions. Published in the United States by Golden Books, an imprint of Random House Children's Books, a division of Random House, Inc., New York, and simultaneously in Canada by Random House of Canada Limited, Toronto. Originally published in 1990 by Western Publishing Company, Inc. Golden Books, A Golden Book, and the G colophon are registered trademarks of Random House, Inc. A Golden Storybook is a trademark of Random House, Inc.
Library of Congress Control Number: 89-82103

ISBN 0-307-12583-1
www.goldenbooks.com

Printed in the United States of America   First Random House Edition 2003

Mom took me to the dentist.
She said I needed a checkup.

DR. GHUM

DENTIST
FOR
SMALL CRITTERS

I didn't need a checkup.
My teeth were just fine.
But we went anyway.

At the dentist's office we met the nurse.
She gave us a great big smile.
I think she was showing off her teeth.

The dentist wasn't ready to see me,
so we sat in the waiting room.

CRITTER
FASHIONS!

Other kids were there, too.
One of the bigger kids had wires
all over her teeth.
Mom said they were braces.
I thought they were neat.
I hoped I would get braces.

We had to wait a long time but there were toys to play with...

...and books to read.

When it was my turn, the nurse
came to get me.

I had to see the dentist all by myself.
But I didn't mind — too much.

We went into a really weird room.
It looked like a spaceship.

I sat in a funny chair.
It was called a dentist chair.
The nurse put a bib on me.

Then the nurse said that she was going to clean my teeth. It tickled a lot.

She told me to spit in the sink.
No grown-up had ever asked me to
spit before.
That was cool!

Next she took pictures of my teeth.
They were called X-rays.
Just like Super Critter's
X-ray vision.

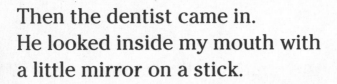

Then the dentist came in.
He looked inside my mouth with
a little mirror on a stick.

The pictures of my teeth were ready. So the dentist called in my mom and we all looked at the pictures of my teeth.

FALSE TEETH
FOR A TIGER

The dentist said I had one cavity
and that he could fix it right then.

They put me back in the dentist chair.
The dentist told me he was going to give
me something so I wouldn't feel anything.

I closed my eyes real tight
and counted to ten.

Before I knew it, the dentist said
it was all over.
I hardly felt anything.

Yuck, then my mouth went numb.
It was weird; I couldn't feel my tongue.

Then the dentist said he was going
to drill a hole in my tooth and clean
out my cavity.
There was a lot of noise in my mouth.
But it didn't hurt.

BUZZZZZZZ

When the dentist finished,
he sent me out to my mom.
The nurse gave me a treat for free.

You know, going to the dentist
wasn't so bad.
It just made me tired.